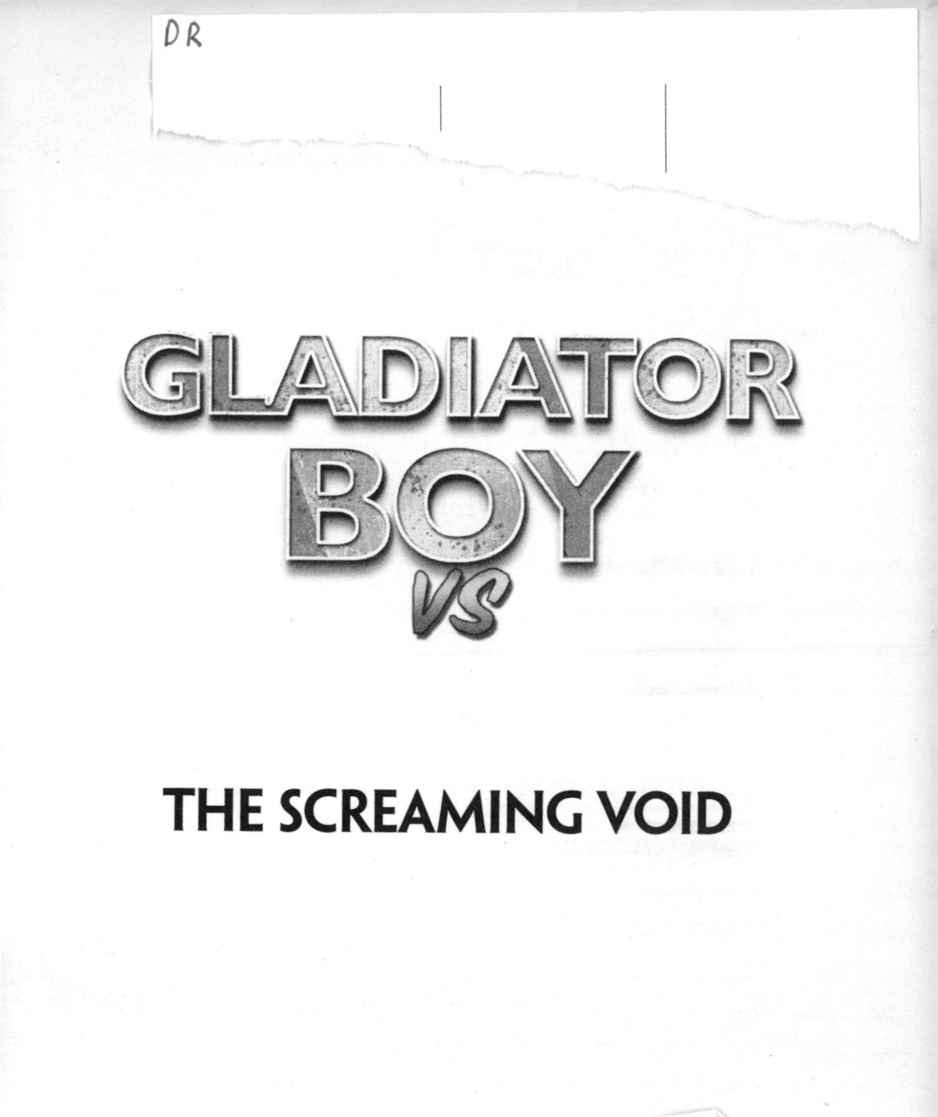

THE SCREAMING VOID

Other GLADIATOR BOY titles to collect:

1. A HERO'S QUEST
2. ESCAPE FROM EVIL
3. STOWAWAY SLAVES
4. THE REBELS' ASSAULT
5. RESCUE MISSION
6. THE BLADE OF FIRE
7. THE LIVING DEAD
8. THE RAGING TORRENT
9. THE THREE NINJAS
10. THE INSANE FURY
11. THE WHITE SNAKE
12. THE GOLEM ARMY
13. THE SCREAMING VOID
14. THE CLONE WARRIORS
15. THE ULTIMATE EVIL

THE SCREAMING VOID

DAVID GRIMSTONE

A division of Hachette Children's Books

First published in Great Britain in 2010
by Hodder Children's Books

1

A Catalogue record for this book is available from
the British Library

ISBN: 978 1 444 90083 5

Typeset by Tony Fleetwood

Printed and bound in Great Britain by CPI Bookmarque, Croydon

Hodder Children's Books
a division of Hachette Children's Books
338 Euston Road, London NW1 3BH
An Hachette UK company

www.hachette.co.uk

For Kim Tallulah Dance and the inhabitants of Hoath.

I would like to dedicate the entire Gladiator Boy *series to Terry Pratchett. There is no writer, living or dead, for whom I have greater respect. Thank you for everything.*

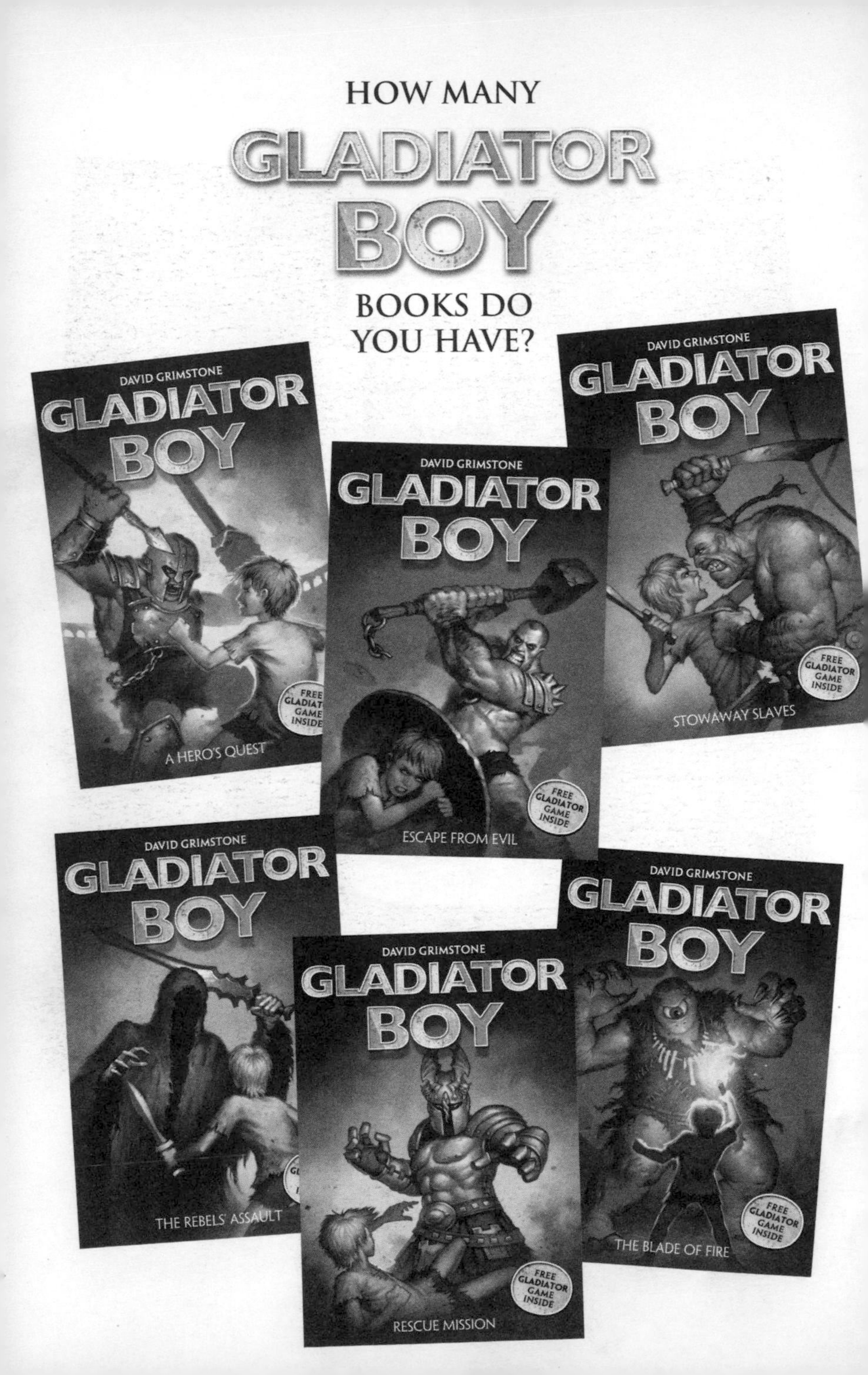
HOW MANY
GLADIATOR
BOY
BOOKS DO
YOU HAVE?
DAVID GRIMSTONE
GLADIATOR
BOY
A HERO'S QUEST
DAVID GRIMSTONE
GLADIATOR
BOY
FREE GLADIATOR GAME INSIDE
ESCAPE FROM EVIL
DAVID GRIMSTONE
GLADIATOR
BOY
FREE GLADIATOR GAME INSIDE
STOWAWAY SLAVES
DAVID GRIMSTONE
GLADIATOR
BOY
THE REBELS' ASSAULT
DAVID GRIMSTONE
GLADIATOR
BOY
FREE GLADIATOR GAME INSIDE
RESCUE MISSION
DAVID GRIMSTONE
GLADIATOR
BOY
FREE GLADIATOR GAME INSIDE
THE BLADE OF FIRE

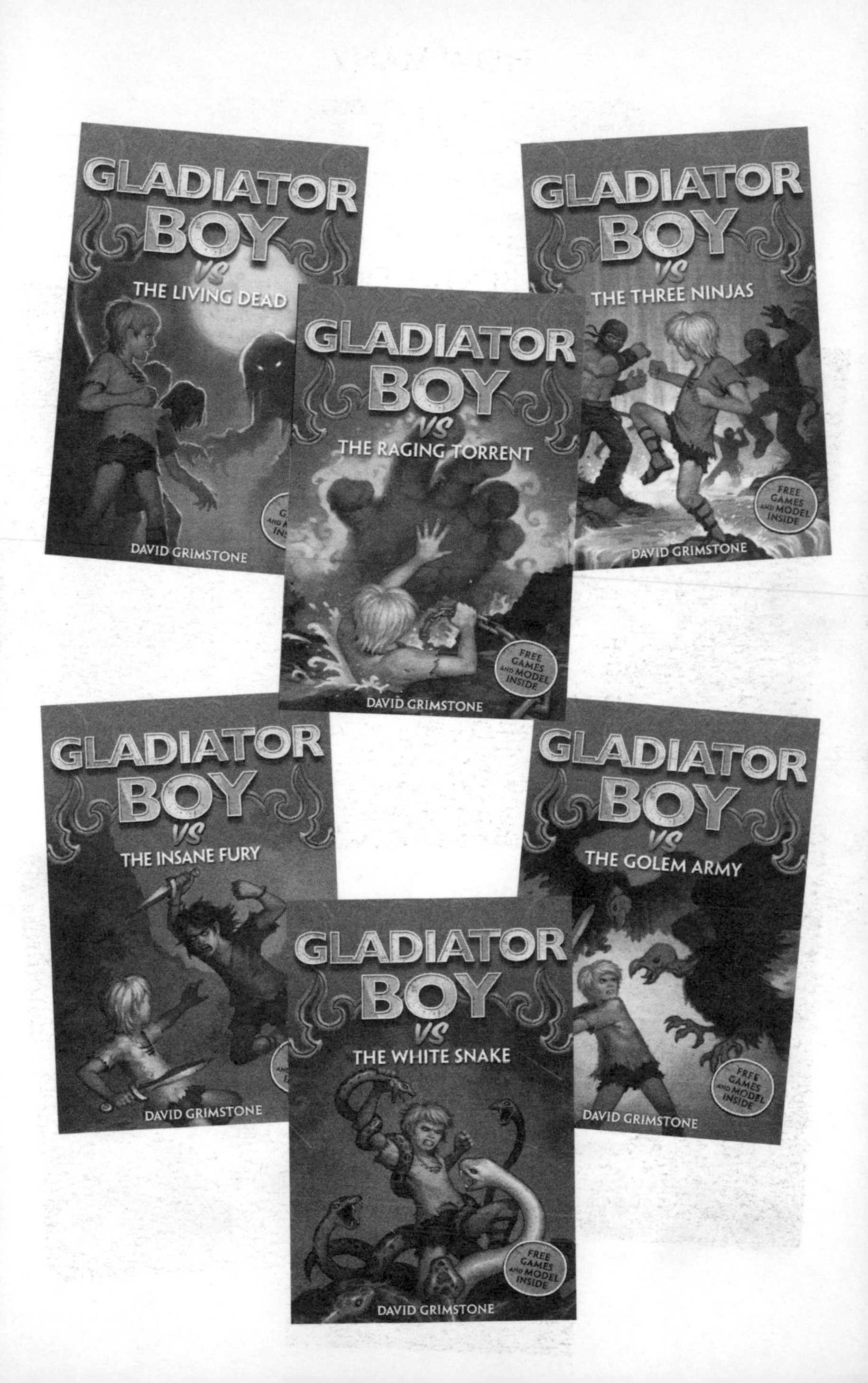
GLADIATOR BOY
VS
THE LIVING DEAD
DAVID GRIMSTONE
GLADIATOR BOY
VS
THE THREE NINJAS
FREE GAMES AND MODEL INSIDE
DAVID GRIMSTONE
GLADIATOR BOY
VS
THE RAGING TORRENT
FREE GAMES AND MODEL INSIDE
DAVID GRIMSTONE
GLADIATOR BOY
VS
THE INSANE FURY
DAVID GRIMSTONE
GLADIATOR BOY
VS
THE GOLEM ARMY
FREE GAMES AND MODEL INSIDE
DAVID GRIMSTONE
GLADIATOR BOY
VS
THE WHITE SNAKE
FREE GAMES AND MODEL INSIDE
DAVID GRIMSTONE

ITALY

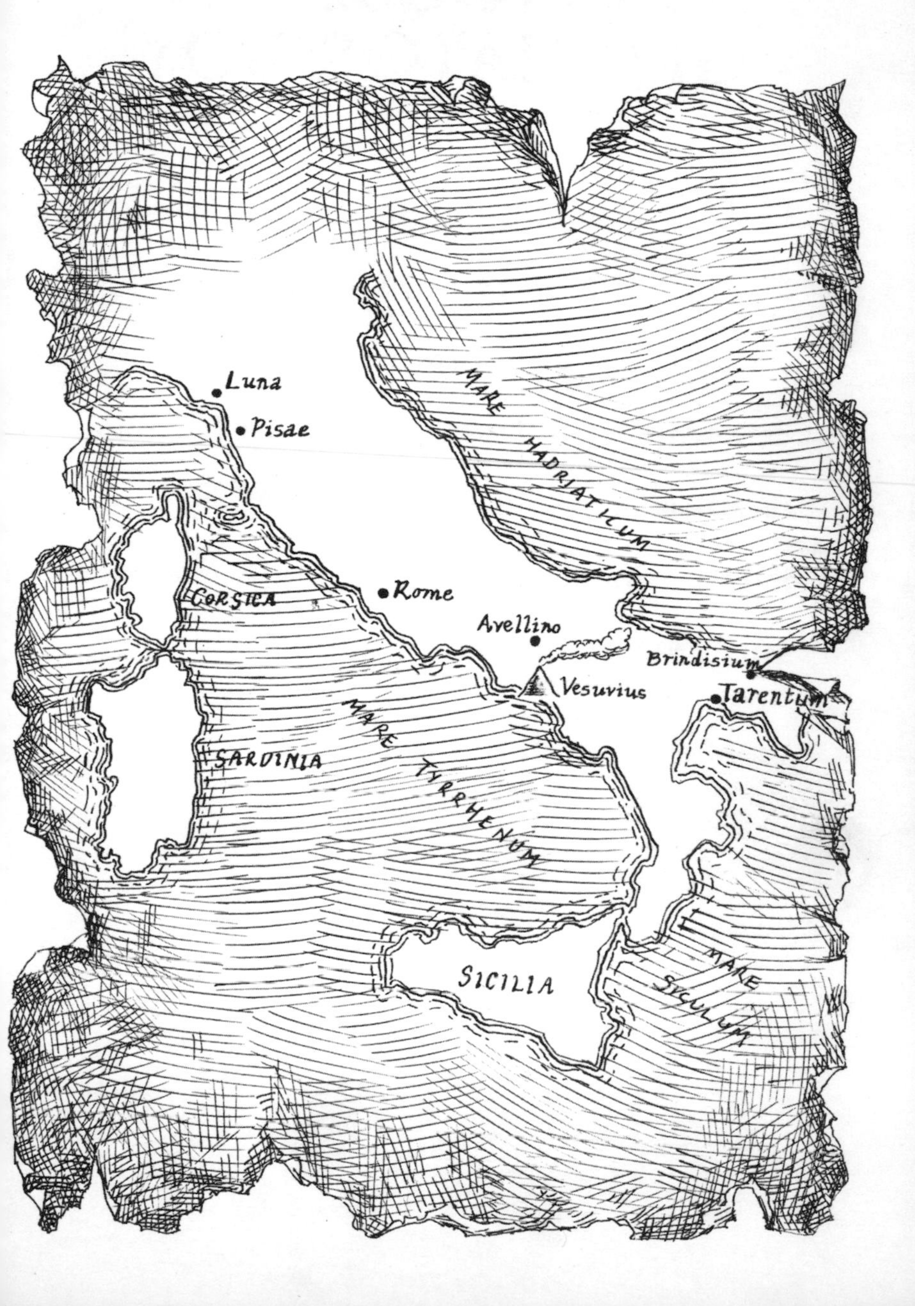
Luna
Pisae
MARE HADRIATICUM
CORSICA
Rome
Avellino
Brindisium
Vesuvius
Tarentum
MARE TYRRHENUM
SARDINIA
SICILIA
MARE SICULUM

PREVIOUSLY IN GLADIATOR BOY

Decimus Rex and his friends have returned from distant Yelang, a province in the heart of southern China. There, they fought and defeated Slavious Doom, and rescued Teo from the palace of the evil King D'Tong. After an intense battle on Pin Yon Rock, the group set sail for home . . . and for freedom.

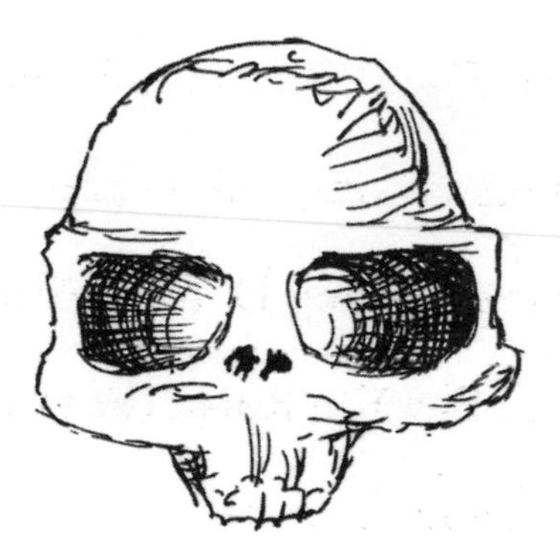

CHAPTER I

A DARK DISCOVERY

The soldiers erupted from the house, hauling their victims across a dusty path and into the small courtyard beyond it. There were only three of them, but they wore the dreaded armour of Slavious Doom's most feared guard unit and displayed the kind of confidence typical of the evil overlord's soldiery. Cackling like hyenas, they suddenly split up: two dragged the beaten man into the middle of the courtyard and forced him on to his knees, while their leader turned his attention to the man's sobbing wife.

'I will ask you one more time,' he said, as a large number of the terrified townsfolk gathered to watch the unfolding spectacle. 'Where . . . is your son?'

The woman could barely speak through her

tears, and her entire body shook as she tried to mumble from cracked and bleeding lips.

'Well,' said the leader, turning to his companions. 'It seems the mother of Decimus Rex is just as difficult to break as her boy. Hmm . . . Captain Lich would not like this, not one bit. We're going to have to cut off one of her husband's hands – maybe that will jog her memory . . .'

As a rumble of mutterings moved through the crowd, the taller of the two guards holding Fenzo Rex drew his sword and snatched at the poor man's left wrist.

The woman screamed out, but the guard leader merely laughed at her.

'You see,' he growled, 'sometimes you have to—'

'I UNDERSTAND YOU'RE LOOKING FOR ME?'

The shout, which was infinitely closer to a bellow, seemed to erupt from all around the courtyard. The crowd instinctively glanced in random directions to find the source of the cry, but the guard leader, who had amazing

perception skills, gazed directly at the roof of the house on the far side of the courtyard . . . where a figure was standing on the roof.

'I AM DECIMUS REX,' it boomed. 'DEFEATER OF ARMIES AND DESTROYER OF YOUR MASTER, SLAVIOUS DOOM. YOU MAKE THE

MISTAKE OF ATTACKING MY PARENTS ON THE VERY DAY I RETURN TO THESE SHORES. A PITY FOR YOU.'

The guard leader squinted at the figure, which was partially obscured by the sunlight streaming all around it.

'So you're the great Decimus Rex?' he shouted. 'And what exactly are you going to do from up there?' He turned to his companions once again. 'He doesn't even have a spear! Hahaha! Hahaahaha!'

It was at this point that the crowd suddenly parted, but the guard leader took no notice. He was still staring intently at the roof opposite.

Gladius threw off the beggar's cloak he'd been wearing and erupted from the crowd like a rogue elephant, slamming into the head guard

with such
force that the
man hurtled
backwards,
crashing
into a pile
of logs
which
subsequently
collapsed on top of him.

The two guards holding
Fenzo Rex threw down
their captive and made
to intercept the attacker as he bore down on
their fallen leader, but they quickly found
themselves surrounded on all sides by a variety
of rough and ragged youths, all brandishing

swords with murderous intent.

'This battle is over,' Ruma snarled. 'If you think otherwise then let's see what you've got.'

'Take your injured master and hobble back to whatever hole you maggots crawled out of,' added Argon, as Olu and Teo both circled the group, warily, their blades at the ready.

The two soldiers charged.

Teo leapt aside to avoid the lunge of the taller man, while Argon swung his sword around in a wild arc and blocked the first three sword strikes he attempted. As the clash of steel echoed around the courtyard, Teo delivered two swift kicks to the small of the soldier's back, while Argon disarmed the man with a twist of his blade and employed a quick head-butt to stagger the man where he stood.

A little distance away, the shorter guard had run into a whirlwind of trouble with Olu and Ruma. The Etrurian attacked with such ferocity that he actually shattered the man's blade on impact, while Olu wrong-footed the guard with a series of well-placed strikes from a small but powerful mace he'd found aboard Tonino's boat.

Gladius watched with increasing delight as both soldiers suddenly lost their nerve, dropping their weapons and rushing to collect their fallen superior, who was weeping on the ground like a very young child with a bruised knee. The big slave grinned.

'Had enough?' he questioned, as the pair managed to lift their chief on to his feet. They were just hobbling away when Decimus arrived in the courtyard.

'Spread the word!' he exclaimed, waving his sword high in the air. 'Decimus Rex and his friends have defeated Slavious Doom and returned to the homeland. Slavers everywhere will learn to fear us!'

As a roar of grateful applause shook the crowd, Decimus fastened his eyes upon two people he had strongly suspected were gone from his life for ever: his mother and father. He ran to greet them, and the crowd slowly began to move away. They knew the difference between a public moment and a private one. The other slaves also stepped away, but Fenzo Rex beckoned for them all to enter the house, an offer which they gratefully accepted.

'We are so very proud of you, son.'

Decimus Rex's father, battered though he was, managed to fight back an ocean of tears as he looked down upon the son he had feared he would never see again. The boy's mother, on the other hand, could not contain her emotions, and was gripping the young gladiator as though she feared he would be snatched away from her even as they embraced.

Around the crude wooden table that served as the only piece of sizeable furniture in the Rex kitchen, sat the other slaves. Olu, Argon, Ruma, Gladius and Teo were all half-drowned with exhaustion: the journey from Pin Yon Rock had taken many days, and left the group feeling crushed in both body and spirit. Only Decimus held on to the determined expression that his friends had come to recognize as a sign of their leader's incredible willpower. While they all thought of returning to their homes and families, Decimus – it seemed – would not be content with his own homecoming until certain questions had been answered.

He broke away from his mother's all-engulfing bear hug, and immediately turned to his father.

'Slavious Doom is dead,' he muttered. 'His army lies in ruins all over Pin Yon Rock, and his henchmen and followers are defeated. But I must know, father: how are things here? Having seen what happened earlier, I'm guessing Doom's men haven't disappeared in his absence?'

Fenzo Rex took a long time to answer, aware as he was that every boy in the room now fixed him with an expectant stare.

'I'm afraid things are very bad, my boy,' he said, his face creased with worry. 'Your escape from Doom has given hope to slaves all over the lands, but I'm sorry to say that by killing the overlord you have merely severed one head from the hydra: Doom's men have acquired new leaders in his absence, and the slavery of children continues. If anything, son, it is far worse than it was before. Hundreds are missing, feared dead.'

'Who is leading Doom's men now?' Gladius asked, his big face contorted in horrified surprise. 'I mean, we've already seen the end of Drin Hain, King D'Tong and that hulking ogre, *Groach*; how many more apprentices can Doom have?'

'Rumour calls him the Mirror Master,' said Fenzo, gravely. 'I don't know if he was ever Doom's apprentice, but it is said that the overlord called upon him in times of crisis. According to what little the common people know, he dwells in a hidden fortress, deep in the mountains . . . but few have actually seen him.'

Decimus frowned. 'Then how . . .'

'He gives his orders through a soldier called Captain Lich; a terrible, black-hearted fiend who looks like death itself. He has sallow, sunken skin and is so painfully thin that many believe him to have already travelled beyond the grave . . . and back. He has a wooden splint in place of his right leg and only a single arm, yet he commands Doom's men with total savagery.'

'Enough of this!' The cry had come from

Decimus's mother, who now rounded on her husband with a fury in her eyes. 'The boy has not been back a day; we will feed him and his friends before they have no strength left to stand! Only *then* will I allow you to fill their heads with all your . . . dark news.'

A terrible silence descended on the room as, her eyes still brimming with tears, Decimus's mother set about finding food and water for her tired guests.

Eventually, their hunger satisfied and their thirst quenched, the boys' concerns resurfaced.

'You said hundreds had gone missing,' Olu prompted, as Argon and Ruma exchanged worried glances.

Fenzo nodded. 'Captain Lich snatched more than two hundred children from the coastal towns. He marched them west in two great snaking lines, all chained together like animals.'

Gladius risked a peek at Decimus, whose lips were already curled in a grimace.

'So what happened to them?' Ruma asked. 'They were headed to another arena?'

Fenzo shrugged. 'Everyone thought so . . . and then they simply disappeared. Two hundred children and the dozen or so men leading them; completely vanished.'

'No one vanishes,' said Decimus, shaking his head. 'Where exactly were they last seen?'

'A soldier heading back to Brindisi on leave reported seeing the group near the heartlands, not far from the Screaming Void.'

These words drew blank stares from Olu, Teo, Argon and Decimus, but both Ruma and Gladius looked up immediately.

'The Screaming Void?' they exclaimed, together.

Decimus looked from the pair to his father, and back. 'What's that?'

'It's a vast and treacherous chasm,' Fenzo continued, leaning back in his chair and shaking his head, sadly. 'It's said to be deeper than the ocean, and local legend has it filled with the ghosts of poor souls who've made the unwise decision to try to find out whether or not that's true. It's called the Screaming Void, because often the last thing heard from those who venture too close to its edge is a tortured scream.'

Decimus took another mouthful of water, and gulped it down. 'Then that's where we start looking,' he muttered. 'A place that people *already* fear is the perfect place to hide stolen children.'

Every head in the room turned to face him.

'You are not getting involved!' his mother shrieked. 'You've been taken from me once, already, my boy – I cannot face the thought of losing you again!'

Decimus Rex got to his feet and looked at his parents with a mixture of love and regret.

'I am sorry, mother,' he said, slowly. 'But I will not stand by and see hundreds of other families suffer whilst I do nothing. My friends are free to return to their own homes, but I am going to find those captured children. If Doom couldn't stop me himself, then no minion of his will stand in my way.'

An infectious smile that started with Gladius travelled around the room.

'What do you say, boys?' Ruma intoned. 'One last mission, to avenge all those who fell under Doom's boot at Arena Primus?'

'I'm in,' said Olu.

'Me too,' Argon added.

Gladius's grin was threatening to consume his entire face. 'And me.'

'I come,' Teo said, his slight voice and speedy nod causing most of the others to laugh out loud.

Decimus folded his arms and grinned widely at his companions.

'Then may the gods smile on Captain Lich and his band of armed cowards,' he said. 'Because that snivelling wretch will need all the help he can get.' He turned to Fenzo. 'We're going to need a new set of swords, father; the very best you can get your hands on. We'll need rope, too – and probably some torches, if the legends about the Screaming Void are to be believed.'

Fenzo Rex stared proudly at his son, and

even managed a weak smile. 'Will there be anything else I can get you, boy? A warhorse, perhaps? A sailing ship?'

Decimus beamed back at him. 'Just talk to Gladius,' he muttered. 'If we need it, you can bet he'll think of it.'

CHAPTER II

THE IMPOSSIBLE SIGHT

The group set out the next morning, following a crude map Fenzo Rex had drawn on a scrap of parchment. Despite this lack of clear direction, the route wasn't difficult to determine.

'It's just one straight road,' Gladius observed, peering at the map over Decimus's shoulder.

The young gladiator nodded. 'For the next few miles, at least,' he said.

'I hope we're in time to save them,' muttered Olu, eyeing the grim rain-clouds that gathered over the hills ahead of them.

Ruma and Argon were both quiet. The group had had a long discussion the night before, debating whether to get involved in another clash with Doom's evil army. Quite naturally, Olu and Teo had sided with Decimus: neither boy had close family in Italy, and both were being cared for by relatives instead of parents. Decimus insisted this fact made no difference to their decision to follow him, but Argon and Ruma felt differently. They both had parents who were desperately awaiting their return . . . and going off on yet another wild adventure would delay that moment considerably. In the end, they had agreed to rescue the other slaves and put an end to Doom's remaining disciples . . . once and for all.

Minutes turned into hours, and the group began to notice a souring of the land: trees that were usually lush and heavy with leaves at this time of year had become deformed and twisted husks, and a cold wind was ravaging the land.

As the group finally left the main road and headed through a thin, almost barren forest, they noticed that the once beautiful countryside was growing ever more depressing. It was almost as if a terrible sickness had blighted the land.

'It's Doom's men,' Gladius growled. 'When I was back in Arena Primus, I heard stories about them burning things: forests, villages, every type of landscape they passed through. It's as if they don't have the intelligence to do anything but destroy.'

The group walked on in silence for a time, none of them feeling the need to point out that the area they were passing through seemed cold and desolate, and mostly consisted of devastated ruins.

They had just climbed a rocky ridge when Gladius suddenly held up a hand to halt their progress.

'Wait! Is that Manduria down there?'

The group squinted at the distant settlement, and Decimus nodded. 'It must be – there are no other sizable towns on this map.'

Gladius shrugged. 'Then we must have passed the Screaming Void, already somehow . . .'

'What?' Argon exclaimed, his voice edged with humour. 'You're telling me we actually walked right past a place called the *Screaming Void*?'

Even Decimus smiled at this.

'Maybe it doesn't scream that loudly,' said Olu, as Teo and Ruma both laughed.

Only Gladius wasn't involved in the joke: he was staring behind him with a sudden, knowing look on his face.

'I saw it,' he muttered.

Decimus was still shaking with mirth. 'What did you say?'

'I actually looked right at it, earlier – just beyond the forest. I didn't realize what I was seeing! It's camouflaged, Decimus: the whole thing is completely covered over!'

The big slave turned on his heels and ran back along the path; the others quickly pulled themselves together and made to follow him.

Decimus gawped at the Screaming Void.

It was an impossible sight, when you finally understood what it was you were looking at: it was like a trick painting where things were not quite as they seemed. On first inspection, the entire expanse of land simply looked like the site of some terrible destruction. Hundreds of the spindly, crooked trees lay criss-crossed on the ground, covering an area so vast that it almost filled the view in every direction. It was only when you stared at the trees for a long time that you realized they were growing out of the ground *horizontally*, filling an enormous chasm that remained completely unseen due to the incredible net of decayed foliage that covered it.

'I can't even see a *gap*,' Decimus muttered. 'How would those soldiers ever have led two hundred children down there?'

'They went missing *around* here,' said Ruma, shaking his head. 'This might not be the actual spot where–'

'It *is*,' said Decimus, defiantly. 'ALL the trees around here are burned and damaged . . . apart from the ones covering this hole. It's a lair of some kind: I feel it in my bones.'

'At least we now know why they call it a *Void*,' said Gladius, evenly. 'I bet the space under that lot is enormous, and pitch dark: I bet there's not even a sliver of daylight.'

'We need to find a weak area,' Olu said, bravely stepping out on to a thick tree trunk and moving halfway along its length. 'There must be a place where the branches are thinner, surely.'

Decimus nodded, as the others began to edge their way on to the roof of the chasm. They each took a different direction, and spread out like a family of spiders on an enormous web.

'We need to be *careful*!' Gladius called. 'The further we get from the edge, the bigger the drop: that's just common sense.'

'So it would be really bad news if the weakest section turned out to be *right* in the middle?'

They all turned to Olu, who was crouching down at what would have been the very core of the chasm roof. The nervous smile he was sporting told the group everything they needed to know: a way in had been found, but it was an extremely perilous one.

As the group gathered around the hub, Olu started to snap off twig-like branches and some of the weaker foliage that covered the area. In no time at all, a small hole had been made: Decimus reckoned it to be about the size of a cannonball.

'Let's make it bigger,' he said, reaching down and yanking away some extra branches. 'There's a heavy rock over by the edge of the tree line, and I want to drop it down there. We need to know how deep this chasm is.'

A few seconds later, Gladius and Argon both hauled the half-boulder towards the gap. Olu, Teo and Ruma helped them make the last few feet, while Decimus crouched low to the hole in preparation to listen to the resulting crash.

'One, two, three – now!'

The boulder slammed through the gap, snapping off several more branches as it plunged into the inky depths of the Void.

Decimus waited, almost holding his breath as second after second began to expire. Then he looked up at the others, who shared his increasing dismay.

'Nothing,' said Gladius, eventually. 'It's a long, long, *long* way down. The chasm must be absolutely huge.' He knelt down beside his friend, and ventured: 'I was thinking . . . that it might be an idea to burn it. If we do that, the sunlight will stream through . . .'

Decimus shook his head.

'No, I wouldn't do that,' he said. 'I know it's the quickest way in, Gladius, but we're not going to be just like them. Destruction is *their* way, not ours. Besides, if we create a massive fire and open up the chasm, it announces our arrival to whoever might be waiting for us down there. If the kidnappers are hiding out in the Void, I want our attack to be a complete surprise.'

Gladius clambered to his feet, and nodded. 'The rope it is, then,' he muttered. 'Does anyone fancy volunteering to go down first? I'll make a small fire for our torches.'

A short time later, Gladius and Argon had become firm anchors for the rope, their feet wedged into the stronger branches of the trees and their stomachs encircled by several layers of the thick line. Teo and Ruma both held fast to the rope in different places, ensuring that grips were clamped evenly along its length.

Finally, Olu crouched beside the hole, a torch raised above his head. He looked incredibly concerned.

'Surely four pairs of hands could support the weight of two of us . . .'

'I'll be fine,' Decimus said, picking up on his friend's worried tone. 'Just give me the torch and get them to lower me as slowly as possible. When I reach the ground, I'll tug three times on the rope. OK?'

Olu nodded, and muttered something under his breath. Then he handed the torch to his friend and signalled for the group to begin letting out the rope.

Slowly, Decimus disappeared into the gloom,

his torch sputtering above him as it threw up glimpses of the occasional rock formation and the outlines of decayed vegetation that invariably clung to every surface. The flames were conspiring with the dancing shadows to make the Void look even more menacing than it undoubtedly was. Decimus swirled the torch around him, trying to make out the edges of the world he now found himself being lowered into.

Above ground, Gladius and Argon were getting nervous. Being furthest from the hole, they were both eager to know what was happening, but the continued silence from Teo and Ruma suggested that even if Olu *could* see something, he wasn't letting on.

'Well?' said Argon, eventually. 'What's going on?'

Olu leaned over and peered into the hole. 'I don't know,' he said. 'He's too far down. I haven't seen him for a few minutes. I think I can still see a distant light that might be the torch, but . . . I'm not sure.'

A vague feeling of unease had settled on the group.

Olu looked up at Teo and Ruma. 'Do you think perhaps we should g—'

It happened so fast that no one really saw clearly *what* it was that had attacked Olu. One second, the young slave was crouched beside the hole, the next he was being dragged into it.

'Arghh! Help me! Arghghhh!'

Gladius and Argon instinctively rushed forward, but skidded to a halt as the rope in their grasp tightened and the recollection hit them that Decimus was probably still dangling from the end. They couldn't afford to move an inch: it was all down to the others to save Olu.

Ruma and Teo hurtled forward in a mad panic. Ruma stumbled and crashed through a network of branches, embedding himself up to the waist. Only Teo moved with enough speed, skidding

across to the edge of the hole and snatching hold of Olu's arms as the very darkness below seemed to consume him.

'Arghhhh!' Olu screamed, flailing wildly as Teo tightened his grip. The little slave tried to lock his feet in the branches, but he was pulled forward with such force that he had no time to work his way into the gaps. There was another, terrible cry from Olu, who actually disappeared into the Void, dragging Teo with him: only the little slave's legs were now visible outside the hole.

Argon spun around to face Gladius, his eyes wild with fear. 'Ruma's still trapped,' he spat, indicating the struggling Etrurian. 'Can you hold the rope if I try to help them?'

Gladius nodded, and Argon wriggled free of

the line, scrambling over the branch floor to snatch hold of Teo's legs. Screaming with the combined rage of fear and determination, Argon employed his savage strength to haul his friends back into the light. At first, it seemed the Gaul was making a futile struggle against an impossible foe, but slowly, very slowly, Argon began to win the fight. He heaved, and heaved, spit flying from the corners of his mouth and a thin film of sweat covering his brow.

First, there came Teo – moaning but still in one piece – and, finally, Olu. The thin slave was barely conscious as he was withdrawn from the Void, and his legs were covered with deep, bleeding gashes.

'He-lp me,' Olu managed, his last words before he passed out from the shock of the event.

A few feet away from where he lay, Ruma wriggled out of the collapsed section that had temporarily claimed his legs and dragged himself back on to the tree floor.

'Get Olu somewhere safe!' Gladius shouted, still bogged down with the weight of Decimus on the end of the rope. 'Ruma! Stay away from that hole! I'll pull Decimus back up!'

As the big slave moved backwards, slowly dragging the rope out of the hole, Argon and Teo lifted Olu between them and hurried him over to the edge of the tree floor. They had only just deposited Olu on the ground, however, when a frantic cry from Gladius drew their attention back to the middle of the hole.

'Argghh! It's taking Decimus! Quick! Hellllp!'

The coil of rope Gladius had earned with his retreating steps was beginning to unravel. Fast.

Ruma, who was closest to the big slave, barely had time to notice the coils vanishing before the rope was pulled taut and Gladius was suddenly wrenched forward. He collided with the Etrurian, and both were dragged, kicking and screaming, back to the edge of the hole.

While Teo tore up some ragged cloth from his tunic to tend to Olu's wounds, Argon thundered across the tree floor, leapt the gap that had previously claimed Ruma and dived on to the back of Gladius. Catching hold of the big slave's generous waist, he strained every muscle in the attempt to halt their forced progress. This time, however, the Gaul's efforts just weren't enough.

'Teo!' Argon screamed. 'Teo! Help us!'

The little slave abandoned Olu and flew across the chasm, moving with such speed that he was almost a blur, to the struggling line of slaves.

Thinking quickly, this time, Teo decided to wedge his feet into the tree network *before* he took hold of Argon's legs, giving him a greater platform from which to drag back the others. It might have worked, but no one could tell because, at that moment, the rope went completely slack.

Gladius flew back, crashing into Argon, Ruma and Teo as he cannoned away from the hole at a violent speed. All four of the slaves ended up in a crushing heap. As the stunned friends tried to regroup, Teo scrambled out from beneath the pile and hurried over to the rope. Snatching it up in both hands, he began to frantically haul it in. After a few seconds, he was joined by Argon, and together they retrieved the end of rope from the chasm of the Screaming Void.

It was covered in blood, and Decimus was gone.

CHAPTER III

THE MIRROR MASTER

Decimus awoke, cold.

At first, he thought he was alone and lying completely still. Then, as his senses brightened, he realized he was wrong on both counts. He was being carried along by a number of clammy hands, each sporting ragged fingernails that dug painfully into his flesh.

He tried to speak, but found that his mouth was stuffed with a cloth of some sort. He tried to struggle, but each time he did, more of the hands snaked out of the darkness and clamped hold of his limbs.

Realizing that resistance was, for the time being, a waste of his energy, Decimus relaxed, allowing his head to loll back as if he had fallen into unconsciousness once again. When he did this, he saw the torch he'd been carrying. It was now being held aloft by an extremely ugly brute of a man who looked exactly like the primitive cave-dwellers he'd heard about when he'd occasionally stopped to listen to the scholars in the old town square. The man had a high, thick forehead and walked with his mouth gaping open, as if was permanently shocked by everything he saw.

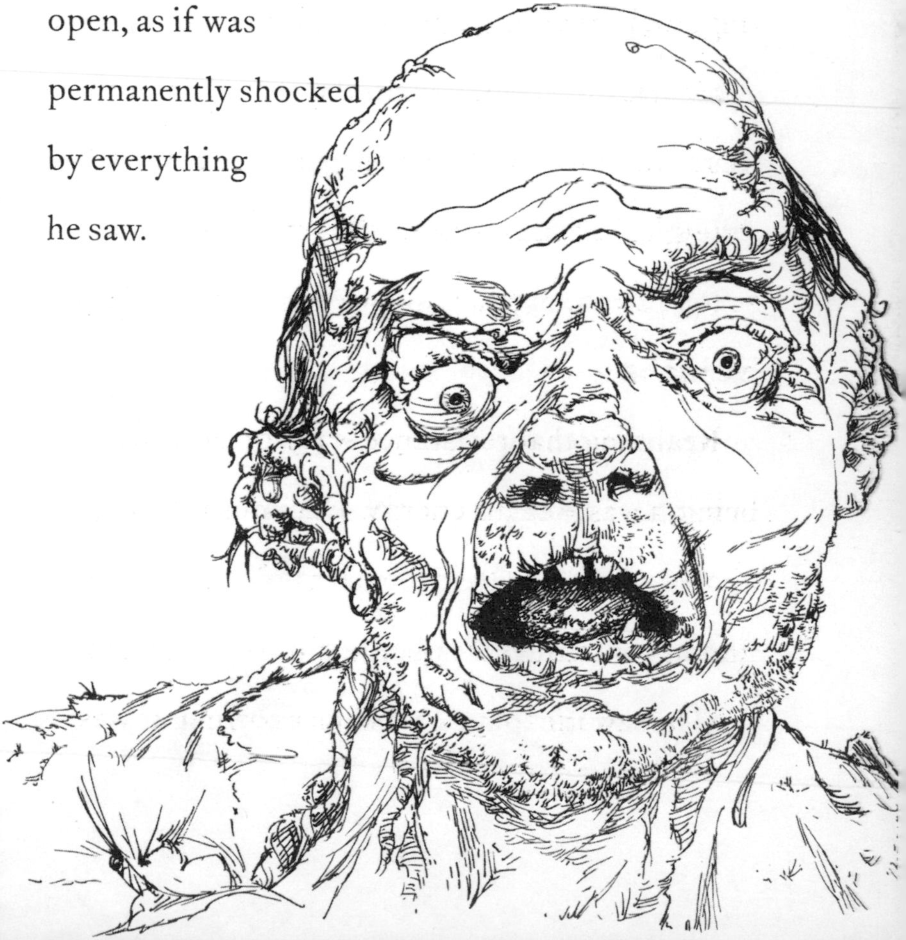

All around him Decimus could hear low grunts and growls, presumably uttered by the others who held on to him so tightly.

It had long been rumoured that wild men dwelt in the hills, tribes of forgotten warriors undisturbed by time and too primitive to be of interest to the Emperor. Judging by the strength of their grip, he reflected, they probably climbed up and down the chasm walls like spiders, waiting near the underside of the tree floor to snatch unsuspecting travellers who ventured too near their lair. If Slavious Doom's men *had* taken the children into the Void, they must have encountered these dark-dwellers or – worse – had managed to control and use the beasts for their evil purposes in some way.

The thought gave Decimus a second wind,

and he suddenly convulsed, kicking out with his arms and legs at the same time. This new attack seemingly took the tribe by surprise, and all the grips clamped around his legs were broken.

Springing back, Decimus slammed his head to the left, connecting with a skull so thick that the resulting blow actually blurred his vision for a second. It did, however, cause the beast holding his left arm to let go. He staggered slightly, then swung around and drove a fist into the face of the man on the opposite side of him. There was a low growl, but the grip remained tight and his captor threw a clumsy but powerful punch back at him. Rallying with exceptional speed, Decimus dodged aside and used the man's own momentum to catch him off guard, slamming an elbow under his jaw. There was another grunt, but this time it was followed by a dull thud as the man collapsed.

Decimus let out a relieved sigh, but as he prepared himself for a new assault the torch bearer suddenly padded forward with surprising agility and hit him square on the jaw. The strength behind the blow was such that it knocked Decimus sideways, and he collapsed, hanging by one arm from another tribesman who had reached out to grab him at precisely the right moment.

The torch bearer grunted, and the group hoisted Decimus into the air once again. Then they moved on.

Far above them, a few narrow beams of daylight had begun to peek through the chasm roof.

The glass fortress wasn't named as such because it was constructed entirely of glass, or because it had an unusual amount of windows set into the walls. On the contrary, the building was made almost entirely of stone and had fewer windows than most castles, having been built at the base of a dark and shadowy chasm. The glass fortress was, in fact, named for the incredible number of mirrors to be found within. They hung on every wall, covered every floor and were set in every ceiling, casting so many dim reflections that a single guard, upon visiting the fortress, could be forgiven for thinking that the place was packed solid, when, in fact, he was standing there alone.

It was a cold and terrifying place, but the Mirror Master liked it that way.

Slavious Doom's instructions had been very clear: if ever he was unable to continue his activities for any length of time, it would fall to his oldest and most trusted apprentice to succeed him. The Mirror Master had done just that, and with the help of the trusted Captain Lich, he had managed to cover the lands in a new darkness, bolstering Doom's slave army with children from towns as far north as Luna and Pisae. Of course, there was always the possibility that Doom might not return from his secret business in Yelang . . . but a sensible man would never count the overlord out.

A torch flickered at the end of the hall.

The Mirror Master swept back a lock of his

long, dark hair and allowed himself a smile. Even in a fortress full of misleading reflections, it was difficult not to recognize the approach of Andrus Lich.

The captain was bald, and his skin was stretched so tightly across his face that many thought him akin to an animated human skeleton. In fact, he was just painfully gaunt and thin, and no amount of eating seemed to change the fact. He had lost his left leg at a young age, while fighting a lion in the arena: it had been replaced by a wooden splint that clicked on the mirrored floor. His right arm had been claimed only a year later, this time by the snapping jaws of a crocodile. Life had been cruel to young Andrus Lich, but he had adapted by becoming crueller.

The Mirror Master covered his smile by

pretending to yawn.

'I thought I said I didn't want to be disturbed,' he said.

Captain Lich gave no apology, instead choosing to wipe a grimy hand across his lips.

'It's the cavers, Islaw,' he muttered. 'They've found a boy. They're bringing him here.'

The Mirror Master ignored Lich's use of his actual given name, and tried to focus on his words, instead.

'Can you not just put him on to the wall like all the others?'

Lich spat a wad of phlegm

on to the mirror at his feet, grossly distorting his own reflection. 'This one threw up a fight, Islaw. He even knocked out one o' the cavers . . . and we both know how difficult they are to put down.'

The Mirror Master nodded, and tapped his fingers on the corner of his ornate glass chair.

'Do you think he might be a good match for the Specials? They do need a worthy opponent in order to be properly tested . . . and none of the children we've tested so far have lasted longer than a few seconds with them.'

Lich sighed, and shrugged. 'There's six of the Specials, and only one of him: it wouldn't be much of a test.'

'He came here alone?' the Mirror Master prompted.

'Well, we don' know that,' admitted Lich.

'The cavers are always difficult to understan', but it appears there might 'ave been others with him that got away. So either our primitive friends are gettin' sloppy, or these others were jus' as feisty as the one they did catch.'

The Mirror Master smiled once again.

'In that case,' he said 'all we need to do is wait. Friendship is incredibly important to most children. You may find that–'

Suddenly the throne-room door burst open and a lone soldier came hurtling inside, stumbling slightly on the glass floor as he skidded to a halt.

Captain Lich spun around, and snatched hold of the man by his throat.

'What's your name, soldier? How dare y–'

'The cavers are going mental!' screamed the

guard, his face riddled with panic. 'They're running in every direction, and some of them are even attacking us! It's turning into chaos out there!'

The Mirror Master quickly rose up from his chair.

'I don't understand,' he snapped. 'What's happened, exactly? What has caused this?'

The soldier shook violently, locked as he was in Lich's terrible grasp.

'We're under attack, my lord! The chasm roof is on fire, and it's raining flames and burning wood! Someone is bringing down all hell upon us!'

Lich nodded, slightly, and then drove his head straight into the guard's skull. When the man collapsed in a heap on the mirrored floor, he turned back to his master.

'Pathetic maggot,' he muttered, prodding the guard with his boot. 'What's your orders, Islaw?'

The Mirror Master put his head on one side.

'Get the cavers under control using that *thing* they're all so terrified of,' he said. 'Then send all of the other guards to watch the children. We don't want a mass break-out. If it turns out that our latest captive's friends are responsible for this event, I want them caught quickly and brought before me.'

Lich nodded, curtly, and left the room. The Mirror Master waited for a few seconds, and then summoned another nameless minion from the depths of the fortress.

'Your wishes, my lord?'

'Send a garrison of my best troops to follow and assist Captain Lich. I sense he may have some trouble with these new intruders.'

'Anything else, my lord?'

The Mirror Master thought for a moment.

'Yes. Fetch the Specials from the vault.'

'At once, my lord. How many would you—'

'All of them,' answered the Mirror Master, with a demonic smile on his lips. 'Bring *ALL* of them.'

CHAPTER IV

FLAMES AND FURY

The slaves all gathered around Gladius, who was now standing at the foot of a bonfire that looked as though it might consume the entire landscape. Surprisingly, however, this particular fire was *sinking*, as the foliage and myriad trees supporting it began, very slowly, to collapse.

'I'm not sure this was your best ever plan,' Ruma protested. 'What if it spreads to what's left of the trees around us? We'll end up setting a fire from here to Tarentum!'

Gladius shook his head. 'It's already collapsing,' he said. 'In a few minutes, we should be able to see a way down.'

'What about Decimus?' said Olu, watching the dance of the flames. 'He's down there too, remember?'

Gladius rounded on him. 'Yeah, I remember you being grabbed too – and then whatever took Decimus leaving the rope covered in blood. Let's just take our chances and go with my idea, shall we?'

As Olu muttered a quiet reply under his breath, there was a thunderous roar and a large section of the tree floor collapsed, sending an incredible shower of sparks into the air.

Gladius began to circle the edge of the chasm immediately, running at a solid pace as more and more of the foliage fell inward. The inner depths of the Void were now being revealed: around the walls were hundreds and hundreds of cave-mouths, all opening into the cavern at various levels, and all surrounded by a network of sturdy-looking vines. Admittedly, many of these were now on fire.

'What are you doing?' Ruma shouted after Gladius, his face a mask of fascinated puzzlement.

'I'm looking for a path of some sort! A way down on to the cavern floor!'

The group hurried off after him, but they eventually arrived back at the same spot, severely deflated and gasping for breath.

'That's it, then,' said Argon, his shoulders sagging. 'There *is* no way down.'

Olu shook his head.

'There's no *path* down,' he corrected. 'We're going to have to climb down using the vines on the cavern walls.'

Argon rolled his eyes. 'Are you crazy? They're on fire! Look!'

'Not all of them,' Ruma observed. 'We can still get down – we just have to move fast. I have a feeling those *things* that grabbed Olu came from the caves, and I don't reckon we'd stand a chance if we got into a fight halfway down the side of the chasm!'

'Can't we use the rope?' Argon snapped.

'No use rope,' Teo muttered, his words attracting the attention of the entire group. 'If use rope, they get us all same time.'

'He's right.' Gladius nodded. 'We split up, and we use the vines. Now, come on! Let's move!'

The group scrambled to the lip of the chasm and swung themselves over the edge, using the vines to proceed down the covered walls as sunlight burst through the gloom all around them. It was a sight to stand and behold, but none of the group could afford to take that chance: their combined gazes were all keenly focused on the caves as they passed each one with great care.

Above and around them, pockets of fire

blazed in random patches, some dying away, others flaring up. The entire chasm was bathed in a pale orange light.

Argon was attacked first. The Gaul had made the mistake of shifting his attention from the caves for just a few seconds, and was peering around to check if Gladius was making the climb OK when a lumbering hulk sprang out of the nearest opening and snatched him from the wall like a giant scooping up a child.

Several gasps went up around the chasm as Argon punched and kicked his assailant, driving fast and powerful strikes at the caver, who seemed to glance many of them aside.

The group looked on, powerless, as Argon and the immense beast struggled in the mouth of the cave, raining blows on each other in what was increasingly becoming a wild frenzy.

'Help him!' Gladius yelled, peering around the chasm to see who was closest. 'Teo! Can you get over there?'

The little slave immediately stopped climbing down and started to scramble *around* the walls, dodging several flaming branches as he went. He was halfway towards Argon's cave when an even larger foe exploded from the darkened hole beneath him and leapt on to the vines with a deafening roar.

Teo had the quickest reactions of the group. Even as the caver began to ascend towards him, he was already scuttling away at his top speed, moving over the vines as if he was simply crawling across the floor. The caver knew every single handhold in the wall section and sprang from place to place like the most skilled of hunters, but by the time he reached the vine where Teo *had* been, the little slave was almost at the roof of the cave containing Argon.

The cavers were now appearing from almost every opening, lunging at the group with murderous intent and howls of demented rage.

Olu was using his long legs to make several

dangerous jumps around the cavern walls, while Ruma had adopted the tactic of making for the nearest cave that appeared to be *unoccupied*.

Gladius knew he was the most vulnerable of the group. Bigger and slower than all of his friends, he would stand little chance of evading the emerging beasts if one made a determined scramble for him.

Reaching a decision, Gladius quickly drew his sword and slashed madly at the vine he was clinging to. Separated from the wall, it weakened, quickly losing its battle against the bulk of Gladius's considerable weight. The big slave flew into the chasm like a dart, screaming as he plummeted and holding on to the vine with every ounce of strength he possessed. He flew through smoke and fire, past cave after

cave and amidst a sea of hairy arms that snaked out to grab him at each new depth he reached. Fortunately, he was falling too fast to be easily stopped and all attempts to halt his progress failed miserably. At length, the vine began to shudder as its lower roots were ripped from the walls, slightly slowing Gladius's journey, but the end was still painful. The big slave crashed into the floor of the cavern, and cried out as a sudden wave of pain washed over him.

He tried to move, but the agony spread from his shoulder to his leg in one swift movement and all he managed was a weak slide on to his stomach.

Far above the struggling Gladius, Teo had joined Argon in his fight to escape the caver's attack. The little slave had leapt on to the beast's shaggy back, hammering a series of short chops into his neck while Argon delivered some of the heaviest and most powerful punches he'd ever summoned up. Not surprisingly, the caver was beginning to sag, folding under the pressure of the double attack . . . but his companions were nearly at the cave mouth, scrambling over the vines like insects closing on their prey. Two of the brutes broke off from the main attack in order to go after Olu, who was still managing to evade even the stealthiest of the cavers.

Then it happened.

Olu made one jump too many, just as the vine he was leaping to caught fire.

'Arghghhh!'

The gangly slave dropped like a stone down a well, glancing off the wall in several places as he picked up speed.

'Olu! Noooo!'

Ruma moved without thinking, ripped a vine from the cavern wall and leapt after his friend. It was a brave gesture, but foolish – Olu was already too far down, and way beyond his reach.

The boy's despairing screams echoed all around the chasm walls.

Olu was snatched just as he fell past the last line of caves, by two pairs of heavy arms that half caught, half dragged him into the shadows. There was the briefest of struggles before poor Olu, still shocked and dazed by the fall, was bludgeoned into unconsciousness.

Teo and Argon were fighting a losing battle. Having finally overcome the heavy, mindless caver who had emerged to attack Argon, they were nevertheless beset by three more of the beasts as they attempted to climb back out of the hole. A quick rain of blows saw both slaves hanging limply in the arms of their overpowering enemies, and the cavers roared with delight.

The base of Ruma's vine snapped free from the

wall at the very last moment, leaving the Etrurian with only the smallest of drops before he hit the hard floor of the chasm. Ruma rolled over as soon as he met the ground, springing back to his feet with incredible dexterity as he peered up into the gloom, trying see what had become of Olu.

'Ruma! He-lp!'

The Etrurian spun around to find Gladius slowly dragging himself across the dusty ground towards him. The big slave was bleeding from a head wound, and seemed to be struggling against great pain in order to stay conscious.

'Don't worry,' Ruma managed, hurrying over to his friend. 'I'll get you back on your feet in no t—'

'RUMA! BEHIND YOU!'

The Etrurian turned on his heel and was hit so hard that his entire body performed an involuntary somersault in mid-air. In all his many encounters with foes both large and terrible, Gladius had never seen such a punch.

Staring down at the Etrurian with a sick smile on his lips, Captain Lich spat a wad of phlegm into the dirt.

'I doubt 'e'll be wakin' up any time soon,' he growled. 'What about you, Fats? You got any fight left in you?' Resting on his splint, he brought a boot down firmly on Gladius's face and then repeated the move on his injured leg, prompting a tortured cry from the big slave. 'Hurts, doesn' it? We got your friend, you know – the one who came down first on the rope. How many more of you are there? Eight? Nine?'

Lich raised his leg splint and drove it into Gladius's damaged knee, twisted it at the last second to increase the pressure.

'Arghghghgh! Arghhghghghghghghgh!'

'HOW MANY MORE OF YOU?'

'Five of us!' Gladius cried, his eyes streaming with tears. 'There's only five of us! Arghhhh!'

'You better be tellin' me the truth, Fats. I don' like liars. Only five o' you, eh? I reckon you're in BIG trouble, then. Big, BIG trouble.'

Captain Lich roared with laughter. Then he sniffed the air, and began to glance around him.

The cavers were emerging from crawl spaces dotted all over the lower walls of the chasm. Several of the larger members of the tribe carried the fallen slaves between them. Through his watery vision, Gladius saw Teo, Argon and Olu brought out and dumped unceremoniously on the ground next to Ruma.

Their prisoners deposited, the tribe then turned to Lich, advancing almost as if they intended to attack the gaunt soldier.

Lich grinned slyly and, reaching up with his single hand, he removed the heavy chain that hung around his neck. Positioned on the centre of the chain was a skull that looked marginally too small and misshapen to be that of a human.

'See this?' Lich muttered, peering down at Gladius with a blank expression. 'It's a dried monkey skull, nothin' more. The red glow comes from a tiny candle burnin' away in the middle. You wouldn' think such a thing would be so powerful, but you'd be wrong. These 'ere cavers are terrified o' it. They reckon whoever keeps the flame burnin' in this wretched thing is a livin' god, an' their lord 'n' master. As long as this flame flickers inside, they'll do ANYTHING I say.'

Lich held the glowing skull above him and all but one of the cavers bowed. The remaining tribe member, the largest and most muscular caver, stepped forward and nodded respectfully at Captain Lich, lowering himself on to one knee.

'Take these wastrels to the fortress an' dump 'em with their friend,' Lich commanded. 'Islaw will want to test 'em all against the Specials.'

The chief bowed his head and grunted an order at the rest of the tribe, who prepared to move off.

Lich wrenched Gladius on to his feet, suddenly aware that the big, wounded slave was mumbling softly under his breath.

'What's that? Somethin' to say, Fats? You want more pain? Is that it? Speak UP.'

'L-lucky and stupid,' Gladius managed.

Lich glared at him. ''Ey?'

'You're lu-lucky and st-stupid,' the big slave stammered, between cracked and bleeding lips.

'Is that right? And why would that be?'

Gladius turned one bloodshot eye on the captain. 'Lu-lucky because you found a way to control these m-monsters . . . and st-stupid because you just told me how you're doing it.'

Before Lich could muster the slightest offence, Gladius blew out a desperate lungful of air . . . and the candle inside the monkey skull flickered and died.

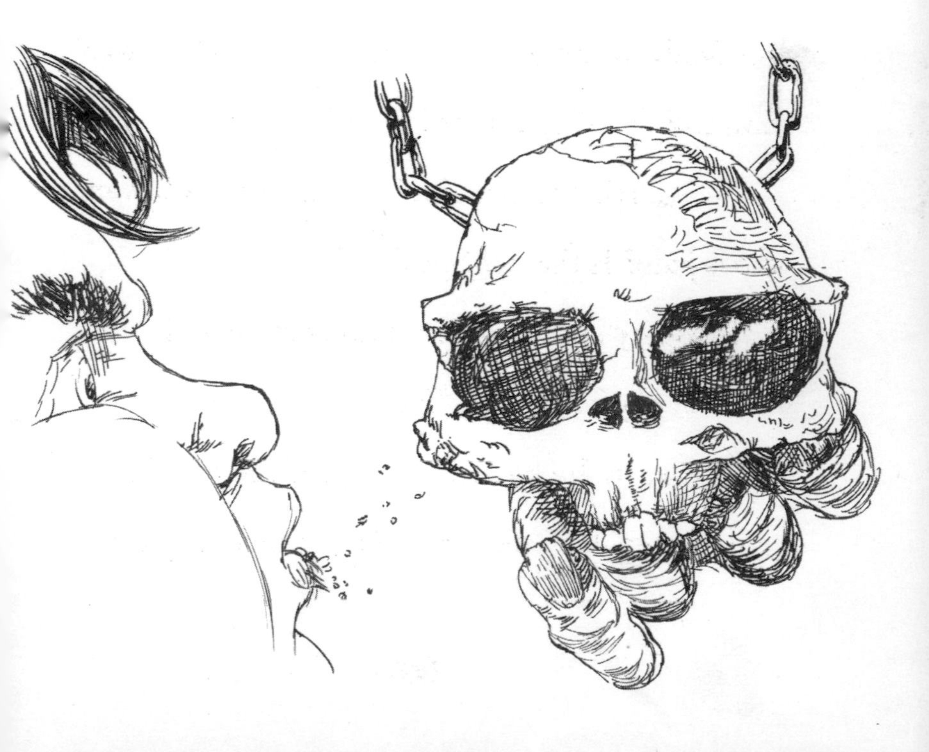

Lich gulped, the chief caver roared and the rest of the tribe erupted into a bellowing horde of chaos.

GLADIATOR GAME

THE FOREST FLOOR

In this game, you must be the first to get safely across the Screaming Void by avoiding the gaps in the forest floor. To play it, you will need two friends, a piece of paper, a pencil, twenty-five coins (any will do, though the larger the better) and two markers/counters (one each to represent you and your opponent; the third person plays the referee and is the chasm itself).

Now, place the coins in five rows of five, and put your markers/counters at one end of the rows (both must be at the same end).

Then the two players must leave the room.

The referee then tears up eight small pieces of paper to place beneath the coins. The pieces of paper must be really tiny, so that they are completely covered by the coins. On four of the pieces of paper, write the letter C (which stands for caver). On the remaining four, write the letter H (which stands for hole). These eight pieces of paper are traps!

Hide the eight pieces of paper under ANY of the twenty-five coins. One rule: you must not completely block a single line or row with traps!

Once this is done, invite your friends back into the room. Then, randomly determining who goes first (the Gladiator game in GB1: A Hero's Quest is a good method), the game can begin.

The first player moves his marker on to the

first coin, quickly turning the coin over to see what lies beneath. If there is no paper under the coin, he stays on that coin and his opponent takes a turn (no two markers are allowed on the same coin). If the paper beneath the coin contains the letter C, the player is immediately snatched below and must start again from the beginning. If the paper contains the letter H, the player gets stuck in a hole between the branches and must miss a turn, allowing his opponent to move ahead!

The winner is the first player to reach the far side and step OFF the final coin. Good luck!

CHARACTER PROFILE
CAPTAIN LICH

NAME: Captain Andrus Lich

FROM: Rome

HEIGHT: 1.9 metres

BODY TYPE: Tall, stooped, rangy

Fact File: Captain Lich has only one arm and a wooden strut in place of his left leg.
Lich is afraid of no one, and while he follows the orders of his superiors, he never treats them with any particular respect. He calls no man his 'master'.
Lich likes to brutalize those under his command, and regularly attacks the junior guards who follow him.

LICH QUIZ: How well do you know Captain Lich? Can you answer the following questions?

1. HOW DOES LICH KNOCK OUT A GUARD WHO BURSTS INTO THE MIRROR MASTER'S THRONE-ROOM?

2. WHAT DOES CAPTAIN LICH CALL THE MIRROR MASTER?

3. WHICH ARM IS CAPTAIN LICH MISSING?

Answers: 1. With a head-butt 2. Islaw 3. His right.

COMING SOON

In the heart of the Screaming Void, the dreaded Mirror Master dwells in a hidden fortress, preparing to test his greatest discovery against the might of Decimus Rex. Meanwhile, a battle rages between the brutish cavers and the dreaded Captain Lich . . . a battle which promises to test the remaining slaves to their very limits.

Will they survive? To find out, read on in the first chapter of . . .

GLADIATOR BOY VS THE CLONE WARRIORS

CHAPTER I

THE BATTLE OF THE VOID

Captain Andrus Lich stood in the middle of a glowing pool of light cast by more than a hundred flaming torches. In one hand he held the battered and bleeding form of Gladius and in the other he held a deformed monkey skull that had, until recently, contained a burning candle. Now, the flame had been blown out . . . and with it had gone the power that Lich had used to enthral the cavers.

The beasts themselves, circling Captain Lich with a rebellious gleam flashing in their eyes, had abandoned their former captives and left the young slaves unconscious on the cavern floor.

Forming a greater circle around the cavers were the newly arrived soldiers of the Mirror Master's guard-army. Swords drawn, they

carefully moved in, eager to save their superior from attack but equally desperate not to start a fight they might not be able to win.

All eyes watched Captain Lich, and the big slave still struggling at his side.

'Stupid boy,' the captain snarled. 'Very, very stupid.'

Gladius licked his bloodied lips. 'I'd say it was smart – now you can't control them, can you?'

Captain Lich released his grip on Gladius, and belted the big slave hard in the face with a ragged fist.

Gladius collapsed, and the cavers moved nearer, their leader beginning to growl as the circle closed in.

Behind them, the outer group of soldiers also shifted towards the captain, slowly drawing swords as the beasts advanced for their master.

Seething in pain from Lich's strike, Gladius rolled over on the ground in front of the dread captain, and suddenly bellowed with all his might: 'CHARGE!'

The cavern exploded with frantic activity.

Certain the order had come from their master, the soldiers immediately flew at the cavers who – in their turn – took the cry as a challenge from Lich. They too lunged forward, and the chasm became a rioting, rampaging battleground.

Amidst the wreckage, Gladius forced himself on to all fours and attempted to scramble between the legs of the warring factions in order to reach his unconscious friends. However, he was trampled and kicked so often that he quickly found a fallen soldier and hunkered down beneath the unfortunate wretch, using his body as a shield of sorts.

Despite having only one working arm and a leg that was effectively no more than a wooden strut, Captain Lich was a devastating fighter. As the cavers charged in, he had drawn his own blade and set about them, spinning impossibly fast and carving his way through the horde without any sign of a controlled strategy. The rampaging soldier was a ball of wild energy, and his decrepit form had apparently done much to disguise the unyielding ferocity he fought with.

His crazed determination instilled the army of guards with a new confidence, and they no longer held back, crashing against the cavers in a storm of blades.

For their part, the primitive tribe fought only with their hands, but they possessed an almost limitless strength. In several places, cavers were actually snatching soldiers off their feet and *hurling* them into each other. Swords flew in every direction, some cast deliberately, some simply released in the whirlwind of combat.

Tortured screams, desperate cries and roars filled the chasm, which was living up to its name as a place of great and terrible suffering.

Then the tide began to turn.

In the end, the cavers were overwhelmed by the sheer numbers of the opposition. Peering out from beneath the crushed soldier, Gladius couldn't tell if the creatures had retreated or fallen in battle: one second the cavern was a tangled mess of furry backs and battered armour and the next it was just the glint of steel and lines of soldiers all standing in battle-ready positions.

Curse the gods, he thought. *That wiry old lunatic has won.*

He'd barely registered the observation when the dead soldier was heaved aside and he was dragged on to his feet.

Two rangy guards grimaced at him.

'Here's the fat one, Cap'n!'

Lich glared at Gladius across what remained of the battleground.

'Good. Now fetch the others and we'll take the lot o' 'em to Islaw.' He kicked the monkey skull into a dusty corner of the cavern. Then he limped over to Gladius and whispered into the big slave's ear. 'Your smart idea just backfired on you. Now those ignorant natives have fled, it's time for you to suffer . . . and believe me, boy, you and your friends *will* suffer.'

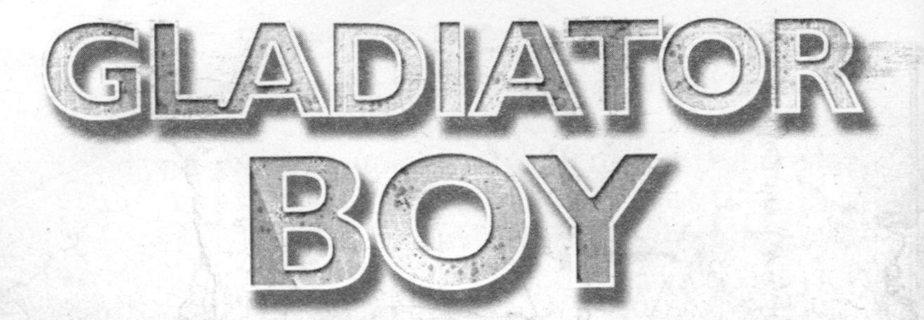

WWW.GLADIATORBOY.COM

Have you checked out the Gladiator Boy website? It's the place to go for games, downloads, activities, sneak previews and lots of fun!

Sign up to the newsletter at **WWW.GLADIATORBOY.COM** and receive exclusive extra content and the opportunity to enter special members-only competitions.